# THE WINNER'S CUP

Adapted by Tracey West

ORCHARD

## CHAPTER 1

# BATTLE FOR THE JADE STAR BADGE

"The battle between the Kumquat Gym Leader, Luana, and Ash Ketchum from Pallet Town will now begin," the gym announcer said. "The Jade Star Badge hangs in the balance."

Ash Ketchum took a deep breath. Luana stood at the opposite end of the large gym.

White lines on the floor marked out the boundaries of the battle area.

Ash had come a long way since he first became a Pokémon Trainer. His journey to capture and train Pokémon had led him to the far-off Orange Islands. Here, Trainers could battle four Gym Leaders known as the Orange Crew to earn badges in the Orange League. So far, Ash had earned three badges: the Coral-Eye Badge, the Sea Ruby Badge and the Spike Shell Badge. Earning the badges hadn't been easy. The Orange League battles revolved around strange tests of skill, rather than the traditional one-on-one Pokémon face-offs he was used to in the Indigo League.

This was his final battle. If he earned his fourth badge, he could go on to compete for the Winner's Cup. Ash wondered what sort of thing he should expect. What kind of twist would Luana throw at him?

"According to Kumquat Gym rules, this battle will be conducted as a double battle," the announcer continued. "Each Trainer will battle with a team of two Pokémon."

Ash absorbed this information. In a typical battle, two Pokémon would battle each other until one fainted. The Pokémon left standing was the winner. But two Pokémon battling together was a different story. Ash knew they'd have to look out for each other. If one of the

Pokémon fainted, the battle would be over.

Luana smiled. The older woman reminded Ash a little of his mother. But he knew she wouldn't go easy on him.

"Have you selected your Pokémon, Ash?" Luana asked. She threw out two red-and-white Poké Balls. "Marowak! Alakazam! I choose you!" she shouted.

The Poké Balls burst open, and two Pokémon appeared out of them. Ash recognised them both.

Marowak was a Ground-type Pokémon that wore a skull mask and used a bone in battle. Alakazam was a powerful Psychic-type Pokémon with long, pointed ears. It carried a spoon in each hand.

Ash's friends Misty and Tracey looked at Ash with concern. Beating a Psychic-type Pokémon wasn't easy. Which two Pokémon

would Ash choose?

"Pikachu!"

His little yellow Electric-type Pokémon was eager to battle.

"I'll use Pikachu, of course," Ash said. "And this one!"

Ash threw out a Poké Ball. A large orange Pokémon burst out.

"Go, Charizard!" Ash cried.

Charizard stomped its big feet and flapped its magestic wings.

Ash smiled confidently. "With Pikachu's electric attacks and Charizard's fire power, I'll be unstoppable!"

Pikachu rushed out to take its place on the floor. Charizard stomped ahead of it, blocking its way.

Angry sparks shot from Pikachu's cheeks. Charizard responded by shooting a stream of flame out of its mouth. Pikachu leapt up to dodge the fire.

"What are you two doing?" Ash cried. "You're not supposed to be fighting each other! We're here to win a badge!"

Ash's friend Misty shook her head. Her orange ponytail bobbed up and down.

"Ash's Pokémon are supposed to work as a team," she told their friend Tracey.

"Ash needs to get his Pokémon under control," the older boy agreed.

But Ash didn't have time.

"Let the match begin!" the announcer blared through the speaker.

"Alakazam, Marowak, go!" Luana yelled.

Alakazam and Marowak both ran to the centre of the gym.

"Charizard, Pikachu, block their attack!" Ash called out.

Pikachu ran past Charizard. The Fire- and Flying-type Pokémon didn't like that at all. It burned Pikachu's lightning-bolt-shaped tail with a hot flame.

"Pika!" Pikachu cried. It held its burned tail and glared at Charizard.

"Stop fighting!" Ash scolded the Pokémon. "Charizard, tackle Alakazam!"

Charizard nodded. It flew across the floor, aiming right for the Psychic-type Pokémon.

"Alakazam, use your Psychic powers to stop Charizard cold!" Luana cried.

A strange light began to glow in Alakazam's eyes. Beams of Psychic energy enveloped Charizard. The Fire-type Pokémon stopped moving in midair. The light from Alakazam's Psychic attack had trapped it.

Ash thought quickly. "Pikachu, help Charizard!" he called out. "Use Thundershock on Alakazam!"

Pikachu hurled an electric blast. It accidentally hit Charizard.

"Chaaaaar!" Charizard roared as its body sizzled with electricity.

Ash couldn't believe what he was seeing. Charizard and Pikachu were supposed to be working together. "Watch your aim, Pikachu!" he yelled.

Luana smiled. "You can't win a double battle unless your Pokémon work together," she said. "Marowak, Bonemerang!"

Marowak threw the bone in its hand. The bone spiralled through the air, then slammed into Charizard. The big Pokémon thudded to the floor, and the bone flew right back into Marowak's hand.

"Now, Alakazam," Luana cried, "hit Charizard with Psychic again!"

Alakazam shot a Psybeam at Charizard, and the Pokémon rose into the air again, surrounded by orange light.

Alakazam looked pleased. It pointed one of the spoons in its hands at Charizard, and gave it a twist. At the same moment, Charizard crashed back to the floor.

Marowak threw another Bonemerang. The heavy bone slammed into Charizard, then returned to Marowak.

Ash looked at Charizard, feeling worried.

The Pokémon was taking a lot of damage. It looked severely weakened.

"Wrap it up, Alakazam," Luana said.

Alakazam raised the spoon again, and Charizard rose up.

Charizard needed help.

"Pikachu!" Ash cried. "Charizard is your friend! You have to help it."

"Pika?" Pikachu sounded reluctant.

Then it looked at Charizard, helpless under Alakazam's powers.

Pikachu nodded to Ash. Electric sparks crackled as it built up a charge. Then it hurled a lightning bolt at Alakazam.

For a split second, Alakazam lost control of its Psychic hold on Charizard. The Fire-type Pokémon landed squarely on its feet.

"Chaaaaar!" it roared. Charizard looked much stronger now.

Luana turned her attention to Pikachu. "Marowak, hit Pikachu with Body Slam!"

Marowak charged across the gym floor, head lowered. It was about to slam into Pikachu when Charizard lowered its huge wing. It knocked Marowak away.

"Pikachu and Charizard are starting to work together," Misty said.

Charizard began to fly across the length of gym, ready to attack Alakazam and Marowak. Pikachu ran alongside Charizard, then jumped up.

"Char!" Charizard paused and let Pikachu jump on to its back.

Ash was relieved. His Pokémon were really working like a team now!

But Marowak and Alakazam weren't giving up. Marowak threw another bone at Pikachu. The Electric-type Pokémon ducked, and the bone missed.

Pikachu responded by zapping Marowak with an electric blast. The attack had no effect.

"Marowak's a Ground-type Pokémon," Misty said. "Electric attacks won't work!"

"This will end it," Luana said, confidently. "Alakazam, Psybeam!"

Ash tensed. A Psybeam could easily knock out almost any Pokémon.

A glowing ball of energy formed in Alakazam's mouth. The ball shot out as a beam of golden light.

"Climb, Charizard!" Ash commanded.

Charizard flew up, just missing the beam. At the same time, Marowak's bone circled back from the last attack. The bone smacked into Alakazam, sending the Pokémon falling forward.

The gym floor absorbed the Psybeam. The beam zoomed across the floor, right in Marowak's path.

Golden light exploded around the Ground-type Pokémon. Marowak teetered back and forth, then fainted to the floor.

"Marowak is unable to battle!" the announcer cried. "Ash is the winner!"

Luana looked out at the battle area, shocked. Then she smiled.

"Congratulations, Ash," she said. "You just won the Jade Star Badge!"

CHAPTER 2

# STUNNED BY VILEPLUME

"I can't believe I earned all four Orange League badges," Ash told Pikachu. He and his friends were resting on a small island.

"Pikachu!" said the little Pokémon. Pikachu was proud of its Trainer.

"That Winner's Cup is going to be mine!" Ash said confidently. "It's the highest honour a Trainer can earn in the Orange League."

Pikachu nodded.

"Let's go and find Misty and Tracey," Ash said. "I bet we can make it to the next island before dark."

Sometimes Ash didn't know where he'd be without his friends. Misty had been travelling with him since he started his Pokémon journey. She got impatient with Ash a lot, and Ash teased her just as much. But they had been through a lot together.

Ash and Misty had met Tracey when they came to the Orange Islands. It happened right after their good friend Brock left them to study with Professor Ivy, a Pokémon Breeder. Tracey kind of invited himself along. Ash didn't mind. Tracey's Pokémon, Marill, Venonat and Scyther, had proved useful in many situations. And Tracey knew a lot about Pokémon.

Ash and Pikachu found Tracey kneeling in a clearing. Tracey brushed a strand of dark hair away from his face. As a Pokémon watcher, Tracey was always looking for Pokémon to study. Today he was sketching a sleeping Vileplume.

Vileplume had a squat, blue body, and a huge red flower on top of its head. In the centre of the flower was a hollow stalk. Ash had seen the combination Poison- and Grass-type Pokémon before, but never one this large.

Excited, Ash ran to his friend. "That's a pretty cool Vile— Whoaaaaa!"

Ash tripped over a rock. He tumbled, knocking into Tracey. The two boys fell into the stalk on top of Vileplume's head.

Vileplume woke with a start. Thinking it was under attack, it pushed Ash and Tracey

out of the stalk. They flew up in the air,
then crashed on to the grass. Then
Vileplume showered them both with a
foul-smelling orange dust.

Ash and Tracey coughed and choked.
Then they fell to the ground. The next
thing Ash remembered, he was lying in a
hut. Pikachu was leaning over him, looking
worried. Misty pressed a cold cloth to his
forehead. He felt like he was burning up.

Ash tried to sit up, but he couldn't.

"I ... can't ... move," he said weakly. His arms and legs felt paralysed.

"You inhaled Vileplume's Stun Spore," Misty said, concerned. "There's no Pokémon Center on this island. I'm not sure how to get you the antidote you need."

Tracey was lying next to Ash. He struggled to talk. "The ... Pokédex," he said.

"Right!" Misty said. She took Dexter, Ash's Pokédex, from his backpack. Dexter was a small computer that held information about all kinds of Pokémon.

Misty asked Dexter about Vileplume's attack. She found out that Salveyo Weed would cure the effects of Stun Spore. Then another picture appeared on Dexter's screen. It was a small, purple Pokémon with a round body, a flat tail and a spiral on its stomach. It was a Poliwag!

"We'll find it!" Misty said. She grabbed Togepi, her tiny Pokémon that still wore an eggshell. She ran to the door.

"Pikachu!" Pikachu wanted to go, too.

"You need to stay here and watch Ash and Tracey, Pikachu" Misty said. "But I'll be right back. I promise."

"Pika, Pika" Pikachu agreed, but it was clearly disappointed.

Misty ran down the sandy trail. "I think I saw a lake when we were out walking before," she told Togepi. "There must be some Salveyo Weed there."

Soon they came to a clear, blue lake that stretched as far as she could see. It would take Misty all day to search the bottom of it.

"How are we going to do this without a Poliwag?" Misty said. "Let's try to find one."

"Togi! Togi!" Togepi chirped.

They didn't have to look far. At that moment, a little purple Pokémon came running through the trees.

"Poliwag!" Misty cried. "Oh, look at its big, round eyes. You're so cute!"

"Togi!" Togepi smiled happily.

But the Poliwag didn't look happy. It hid behind Misty's legs, trembling. Misty saw that it was afraid.

"What's the matter, Poliwag?" Misty asked.

"Hand over that Poliwag!" a voice cried.

Misty spun around. A young man with blue hair came running out of the trees. He wore a white uniform with a red "R" on the front.

Alongside him ran Meowth, a white
Scratch Cat Pokémon.

"James!" Misty cried. James was part of
Team Rocket, Pokémon thieves who were
always chasing Misty and her friends.

"What are you doing here?"

"We want that Poliwag," Meowth said.

"Well, this Poliwag doesn't want to go
with you," Misty replied.

Poliwag whimpered.

Meowth and James looked at each other.

"There's no use being polite with this
Poliwag," Meowth said.

"Right! We'll just have to take it," James
said. He threw a red-and-white Poké Ball.
"Victreebel, go!"

A Pokémon as tall as James burst from
the Poké Ball. Victreebel looked like a
yellow, bell-shaped plant.

Victreebel tried to swallow James.

"Not me," James cried. "Attack them!"

Victreebel spat James out. Then it bounced across the grass, towards Misty and Poliwag.

Misty was ready. She threw a Poké Ball. "Go, Goldeen!" she cried.

CHAPTER 3

# MISTY VS JAMES

A frilly goldfish Pokémon appeared in a flash of white light. Goldeen looked pretty and delicate, but it had a fierce horn on its forehead.

"Victreebel, Razor Leaf!" James commanded his Pokémon.

Sharp green leaves flew out from Victreebel's bell-shaped flower and towards

Goldeen. The Goldfish Pokémon
splashed into the lake to avoid them.

Victreebel jumped off the shore. Goldeen
rose up out of the water, slamming
Victreebel with its horn.

Victreebel flew
up in the air. As it
came down, Goldeen
smacked into the
Grass- and Poison-
type Pokémon
once again.

"Goldeen, Fury attack!" Misty cried.

*Bam! Bam! Bam!* Goldeen jumped out
of the water again and again, each time
smacking Victreebel with its horn.

With one final slam, Goldeen deposited
Victreebel back on shore. The Pokémon was
looking very tired and weak.

James frowned. He held out a Poké Ball.
"Return, Victreebel," he said.

Victreebel disappeared inside the ball.

"Togi! Togi!"

"Poli! Poli!"

Togepi and Poliwag gave a happy cheer.

But James wasn't finished. "Go, Weezing!"
he said, throwing another Poké Ball.

Weezing, a Poison-type Pokémon,
looked like a purple cloud with two heads.

"Weezing! Weezing!" it moaned as it
burst out of the Poké Ball.

Misty didn't miss a beat. "Go, Staryu!"
she cried, throwing a Poké Ball. A five-
pointed Star Shape Pokémon appeared.
Staryu had a red jewel in its middle.

"Staryu, Tackle!" Misty called out.

"Weezing, Tackle," James countered.

Weezing and Staryu flew at each other.

*Slam!* They collided in midair.

*Slam!* Another Tackle.

*Slam!* They crashed into each other again.

"Weezing, Smog attack!" shouted James.

Weezing belched out a thick cloud of black smog. The putrid smoke covered Staryu.

Misty knew what to do. "Staryu, Double Edge!" she shouted at her Pokémon.

Staryu spun wildly around and around, creating a strong wind. The wind quickly cleared the smog.

Staryu spun faster and faster. Then it zoomed through the air and slammed into Weezing.

"Weezing!" The Poison-type Pokémon soared away.

"You did it, Staryu!"

Meowth faced Misty angrily. "I guess it's up to me," it said.

Misty recalled Staryu. She threw out a
third ball. "Go, Psyduck!"

A chubby yellow Pokémon that looked
a bit like a duck popped out.

Meowth grinned. "Getting rid of this
birdbrain will be easy," the Scratch Cat
Pokémon said. "Scratch attack!"

Meowth lunged at Psyduck, its claws
bared. It scratched Psyduck across the face.

"Psy, psy." Psyduck didn't seem in the least
bothered by Meowth's Fury Swipe.

Meowth frowned. "Now I'll use Bite!"
it yelled at Misty threateningly.

Meowth opened its mouth wide and
tried to bite Psyduck's big head.

"Psy. Psy," Psyduck moaned. Its eyes
began to blink rapidly.

"That's it, Psyduck," Misty shouted
encouragingly. "Use Disable!"

Psyduck blinked. A light glowed on its head. Then the light covered Meowth.

"I can't move!" Meowth cried, frozen in light.

"Now use Confusion," Misty told Psyduck.

"Psy-aye-aye!" Psyduck cried. A bright light flashed, and Meowth went careening backwards. It crashed into James. The two fell to the ground in a faint.

Slowly, Meowth and James got up.

"I can't believe we lost to a little twerp like her," Meowth complained.

"All we were trying to do was find some Salveyo Weed to help Jessie," James said.

Meowth and James sulked away.

"Good battle, Psyduck," Misty said, recalling her Water-type Pokémon. "But we

really need to find that Salveyo Weed for Ash and Tracey." Poliwag rubbed itself against Misty's legs affectionately.

"Poliwag, do you think you can do us a favour?" Misty asked.

Poliwag nodded.

"We need to find some Salveyo Weed." She showed it the picture in the Pokédex. "Do you know where we can find some?"

"Poli! Poli!" Poliwag said excitedly. It jumped into the lake.

A moment later, Poliwag swam back with strands of the green plant in its mouth.

"All right!" Misty said.

Misty called on Staryu again. "Let's go!"

Poliwag dived back into the water. Misty held on to Staryu's back as they dived down to the lake bottom. Clumps of Salveyo Weed grew along the sandy floor.

Misty, Staryu and Poliwag gathered as much of the plant as they could. Then they swam back to the shore.

"We've got what we need," Misty said. "Let's get to Ash and Tracey."

Before leaving, Misty placed a pile of the Salveyo Weed on the shore.

"Togi?" Togepi wondered.

"We may be enemies, but I can't turn my back on someone in trouble," Misty said. "Team Rocket can use this to help Jessie."

Poliwag followed them back to the hut.

"Pikachu!" Pikachu was relieved to see them returning.

Misty quickly boiled the plant in fresh

water. She gave Ash and Tracey a cup of the hot liquid.

As the liquid slipped down his throat, Ash could feel the sensation coming back to his arms and legs. His whole body felt cooler. He sat up.

"Sorry it took me so long," Misty said. She told Tracey and Ash about her battle with James.

Tracey sat up next. He noticed Poliwag.

"Looks like you've caught a Poliwag," Tracey said.

"I guess I did," Misty admitted. She turned to Poliwag. "How would you like to come along with me and Togepi?"

"Poli! Poli!" Poliwag said happily. Togepi chirped and gave the Water-type Pokémon a hug.

Ash stood up and stretched his arms.

"I hope your new Poliwag is ready to go,"
Ash said. "I've got a Winner's Cup to win!"

## CHAPTER 4

# PUMMELO ISLAND

Soon, Ash and his friends were riding on the back of Lapras, Ash's large blue Water- and Ice-type Pokémon. An island rose out of the ocean a short distance away. Ash could see a round stadium on top of the island.

"It's Pummelo Island!" Ash said. "Pummelo Stadium is where the battle for the Winner's Cup is held. We're here, Pikachu!"

Pikachu jumped up on Ash's shoulder. "Pikachu!" it said happily.

Lapras was just reaching the shore. Ash was so excited that he ran into town as soon as Lapras was safely back in its Poké Ball. He couldn't wait to get started!

Ash's friends followed him into the Stadium Office. A man with grey hair and a moustache stood behind a counter. A badge on his jacket read *Tournament Clerk*.

"I've come to apply to enter the Orange League," Ash told him. He showed the clerk all four of the Orange League badges he had earned. All four of the badges were shaped like seashells with jewels in the middle. They proved that Ash had defeated the Orange Crew, the four main Orange League Gym Leaders.

The tournament clerk took out a small handheld scanner and held it over each badge. The scanner beeped every time.

"Well, all four badges check out," he said, smiling. "That qualifies you to compete for the Winner's Cup."

"All right!" Ash said.

"Hey, Ash, look at this," Tracey said. In the corner of the office sat a small, stone statue of a Dragon-type Pokémon. "I wonder what kind of Pokémon this is."

The clerk smiled again. "Your match is tomorrow, Ash," he said. "Let me show you and your friends the Palace of Victory."

Ash and the others followed the old man down the street to a round building with a domed roof. Inside, the walls were lined with photos of Pokémon Trainers and stone tablets with Pokémon footprints in them.

"These photos are here to honour those who have won the Orange League Winner's Cup," the tournament clerk said. "In order to enter the hall, you have to defeat the leader of Pummelo Stadium in a full battle."

"A full battle?" Ash asked. "What's that?"

"That's a six-on-six battle," replied the clerk. "Six of your Pokémon against six of the leader's Pokémon. The six Pokémon take turns battling. A Trainer can recall a Pokémon if it gets weak, and use it again later. Of course, if a Pokémon faints, it's out of the battle. The battle ends when all six of one Trainer's Pokémon have fainted."

"That's a long battle," Tracey told Ash. "You'll have to think carefully about which types you'll use."

Tracey pointed to another statue of the Dragon-type Pokémon. "Excuse me, sir. What kind of Pokémon is that?"

"It's a Dragonite," the clerk replied. "The legendary Pokémon that guards this island."

"I knew it!" Tracey said.

Ash took out his Pokédex. "Dragonite, the Dragon- and Flying-type Pokémon," Dexter said. "This extremely rare species is able to fly faster than any other Pokémon."

"Drake, the leader of Pummelo Stadium, commands a Dragonite," the clerk said.

"He does?" Ash asked a little nervously. He'd never battled a Dragonite before. He knew they were pretty powerful.

"No one has won the Winner's Cup since Drake arrived," said the tournament clerk.

"Wow, Ash," Misty said. "You've got a big challenge ahead of you. One of your biggest ever! It's going to be tough."

"You can say that again!" Ash said. "I'd better go and work out a strategy."

The friends headed to the local Pokémon Center. Once they were inside, Ash let his Pokémon out of their Poké Balls.

"Wake up, everybody!" Ash cried.

Charizard appeared and stomped its feet. Then came Bulbasaur, a Grass- and Poison-type Pokémon. Lapras burst out and shot a stream of water from its mouth. Squirtle, a cute turtle Pokémon, squirted water with Lapras. Pikachu joined them by shooting electric sparks into the air.

Then came Ash's sixth Pokémon, Snorlax. The enormous Pokémon was sound asleep.

"Snorlax just had a big meal one hour ago," Tracey reminded him. "It only wakes up when it's hungry. It probably won't wake up in time for the competition."

"You're right,"

Ash said. He put Snorlax back in its Poké Ball. "I'll see if I can get one of my other Pokémon from Professor Oak."

Professor Oak had started Ash on his Pokémon journey by giving him a Pokédex and his very first Pokémon, Pikachu. Because Pokémon Trainers were only allowed to carry six Pokémon at a time, Ash's extra Pokémon were in the professor's care.

Ash explained his problem to Professor Oak over a videophone.

"Are you sure you want to use a Pokémon you haven't used before?" Professor Oak asked. "Pokémon battle better when they know their Trainers."

"I don't have a choice," Ash said. "Besides, you've been training them, haven't you?"

"I suppose," Professor Oak said. He

paused for a
moment, looking
thoughtful. Then
he said, "You could
use Muk or Tauros."

The wild bull
Pokémon walked up
to Professor Oak and
snorted. Ash had caught his
Tauros in the Safari Zone.
He had never used it in battle. But it was
a strong, solid Pokémon. It would make a
good replacement for Snorlax.

"I choose Tauros!" Ash said.

"Great!" said Professor Oak, smiling.
"Then let's make the exchange."

Next to the videophone was a Poké Ball
transfer machine. Ash placed Snorlax's
Poké Ball on a metal platform. White light

zapped it from above. It vanished.

Then more light zapped the platform.
Another Poké Ball appeared.

Ash threw out the Poké Ball. "Tauros, I
choose you!"

The brown Pokémon appeared in a flash
of light. It snorted and pawed its front leg. It
waved all three of its tails.

"That's a nice Tauros, Ash," Tracey said.

"It sure is," Ash said. "And with its help,
I'm going to win the match tomorrow!"

## CHAPTER 5

# DITTO STARTS THE BATTLE

"Pummelo Stadium is pulsing with energy as it welcomes a new challenger," said the announcer. "Not one challenging Trainer has beaten Drake, the stadium leader, since he began his reign of domination. Opposing him is Ash Ketchum from Pallet Town. Will Ash be able to do what no one else has?"

Ash stepped out of a doorway into the open-air stadium. Pikachu walked at his side. Every seat in the stadium was full. A huge statue of a Dragonite overlooked the battlefield. A large scoreboard overhead flashed pictures of Ash and Drake.

A tall, muscular man with black hair stepped out of the opposite doorway. Drake wore a sleeveless red shirt. Around his neck hung a Poké Ball on a chain.

*So this is the guy who can handle a Dragonite,* Ash thought, sizing up his opponent.

The two trainers met on the sidelines, and the large crowd went wild. Ash and Drake shook hands.

"Welcome to the Orange League Winner's Cup," Drake said.

"I'm happy to be here," Ash replied.

A judge in an orange shirt stepped in between them.

"The battle will be six-on-six," he said. "The challenger can switch Pokémon at any point during the battle. And a field change will occur when any three of one Trainer's Pokémon become unable to battle."

"Field change?" Ash asked.

At that moment, the stadium floor opened up. Two halves of the floor split apart, revealing a large pit underneath. A new field rose up from the bottom of the pit. This field was dotted with rocks and huge

boulders. A pool of water shaped like a
Poké Ball sat in the centre.

"The first field will be a rock and water
field," the announcer blared.

Ash studied the field's rocky surface. This
was going to be harder than he thought.

"The battle is about to begin," the
announcer said. "Pay attention to which
Pokémon each Trainer chooses."

Ash and Drake took their positions on
opposite sides of the field. Drake held up
a Poké Ball.

"See what you can do against
my first pick!" Drake said,
tossing the ball in the air.

A pink, blobby-looking
Pokémon burst out
from the ball. It landed
on a tall boulder.

"A Ditto!" Ash exclaimed.

A picture of Ditto lit up on the scoreboard, next to Drake's picture.

"With its one and only technique, Transform, Ditto can turn into any Pokémon the Trainer wishes," said the announcer.

"This is a tough one," Tracey said. He and Misty watched from the first row.

"You're right," Misty agreed. "It won't matter what type of Pokémon Ash chooses at all. Ditto can mimic its opponent's attacks."

Ash wanted to start out strong. He turned to Pikachu. "Pikachu, decide this with a powerful electric charge!"

Pikachu's picture lit up on the scoreboard.

"Pika! Pika!" Pikachu nodded excitedly. It was eager to battle.

Pikachu jumped energetically on to a tall rock. Sparks crackled around its face as it gathered energy for the attack.

"Ditto, Transform!" Drake yelled. White light glowed around Ditto. Its blobby form started to take shape. When the light faded, a little yellow Pokémon stood on the boulder.

"Ditto has taken the form of a Pikachu!" the announcer cried in amazement. "Talk about seeing double!"

Ash understood Drake's strategy. Now Ditto could use all of the attacks that Pikachu could. The two Pokémon would be evenly matched.

Pikachu hurled a huge bolt of sizzling electricity at Ditto. Ditto absorbed the energy. When the attack was over, Ditto looked as strong as ever.

"What was Ash thinking?" the announcer asked. "Responding to an Electric attack with another Electric attack is useless. They cancel each other out!"

Ditto countered the attack with a Thundershock. The huge lightning blast electrified Pikachu. But Pikachu wasn't shaken by the charge.

"Won't these guys learn?" groaned the announcer into the speaker.

But Ash wasn't ready to change his strategy, no matter what the loud-mouthed announcer thought.

"Pikachu, Thundershock!" Ash cried.

Drake followed Ash's lead. "Ditto! Thundershock!"

The two Pokémon aimed jagged lightning blasts at one another.

The two massive bolts met in the air, creating a huge explosion.

The backlash caused the high rock Pikachu was standing on to crumble to pieces. Ditto's rock was falling apart, too.

"Ditto, go with the flow!" Drake commanded his Pokém.

Ditto quickly regained its balance and started jumping nimbly from one piece of falling rock to the next. It landed safely on another tall rock.

At the same time, Ash wasn't sure how to command Pikachu. Pikachu fell to the harsh field below. The lightning mouse looked battered and shaken, but it wasn't out yet.

"Ouch! That's gotta hurt," the announcer said. "Too bad Ash didn't read the field better. He could be losing his cool."

"I am not losing my cool!" Ash shouted.

"Hold it together, Ash!" Tracey called out.

Ash tried to calm down and think of the best strategy to use next. "Ditto is Ditto and Pikachu is Pikachu," Ash said aloud. "There must be some way to beat it."

Drake wasn't taking any breaks. "Ditto, Agility!" he yelled.

Ditto started to run across the rock field, quickly darting back and forth.

"Pikachu, Thundershock!" Ash called.

Pikachu aimed another lightning bolt at Ditto. But it expertly moved out of the way.

"Ditto, Thunder!" Drake countered.

Ditto aimed another Electric attack at Pikachu. Pikachu ducked, missing the blast.

*Ditto is Ditto*, Ash reminded himself. Then suddenly, he knew what to do.

"Pikachu, Quick Attack!" he ordered.

"Ditto, Quick Attack!" Drake repeated, just

as Ash knew he would.

Pikachu and Ditto ran across the field at each other. They jumped high in the air, then slammed together. Electric sparks flew.

"Pikachu and Ditto collide!" the announcer said, as the crowd gasped.

Pikachu and Ditto both fell to the ground. Ditto looked very weak, but Pikachu was still jumping around with lots of energy.

"Now, Pikachu!" Ash yelled.

Pikachu zapped Ditto again with Thundershock. This time, the charge finally took its toll. Ditto changed from a Pikachu back to its own form.

"Ditto is down! Its Transform broke down, thanks to the impact of that collision," the announcer reported.

Ditto reeled back and forth. Then it collapsed in a faint.

"Ditto is unable to battle," said the judge.

"It's goodbye to the little pink guy," the announcer said. "Pikachu wins this round!"

The crowd cheered. Ditto's picture on the scoreboard went dark.

"I get it," Tracey said. "Ditto can copy the attacks of other Pokémon. But when it comes to taking punishment, it's stuck with its own powers. So Pikachu was much better prepared for the collision."

"Good work, Ditto," Drake told his Pokémon. "Return!"

Drake threw out another Poké Ball.

A Pokémon that looked like a huge serpent made of rocks slammed on to the battlefield.

"Drake has chosen an Onix. This Rock- and Ground -type Pokémon is rock solid against Electric attacks. How will Ash respond?" the announcer wondered.

Ash had to think. Pikachu wouldn't do any harm to Onix. He needed a Pokémon that was strong against Rock-type Pokémon.

Which one should he choose?

CHAPTER 6

# ONIX VS SQUIRTLE

"Squirtle, I choose you!" Ash yelled. He tossed out Squirtle's Poké Ball.

"Squirtle! Squirtle!" The Water-type Pokémon jumped up on a rock, ready to face its oppponent.

"Ash is full of surprises," said the announcer. "Squirtle looks like a speck on the field compared to Drake's mighty Onix. Ash has a rocky road ahead of him if he wants to win this round."

Misty defended her friend. "Water-type Pokémon are actually always good against Rock-type Pokémon."

"Don't forget," Tracey reminded her, "if Drake's Onix has a lot of experience, it might have an advantage."

"Squirtle! Water Gun!" Ash called out.

"Onix! Dig!" Drake countered.

Squirtle shot a powerful jet of water from its mouth. If it hit Onix, the Rock-type Pokémon would surely go down immediately.

But Onix leaped up and dived headfirst into the dirt. It burrowed into the field and quickly disappeared. The Water attack completely missed it.

The ground began to rumble. Squirtle looked around nervously. It knew Onix was somewhere underneath. But where?

"After using Dig, Onix is sure to attack from underground," the announcer said. "Squirtle had better look out below!"

"Squirtle, dive into the water!" Ash told his Pokémon. "You'll be safe there!"

Squirtle ran as fast as it could to the Poké Ball-shaped pool in the centre of the field. Rocks rumbled around it as the ground shook harder and harder.

Soon the pool was in sight. Squirtle jumped up, ready ...

"Onix, now!" Drake yelled.

Onix burst through the ground, towering in front of the tiny Turtle Pokémon. Squirtle landed on Onix and ran up the Pokémon's long neck. Ash knew that Squirtle was still trying to find a way to dive into the pool. *It just might make it,* he thought.

"Onix, Bind!" commanded Drake.

Squirtle tried to jump off Onix's back. But Onix wrapped its snake-like body around Squirtle. The Water-type Pokémon was wrapped tightly in Onix's tail.

"Squirtle can't get away!" the announcer cried. "Now Squirtle can't use its signature Water Gun attack! This turtle's in trouble!"

Ash thought quickly. He had to make sure Squirtle didn't get hurt.

"Squirtle! Withdraw and protect yourself!" Ash told his Pokémon.

Squirtle pulled its head, arms, and legs into its strong shell.

"Give up?" Drake asked. "Your Squirtle can't do much in that position."

Ash shook his head. "No way. No matter

how fast it is, a Rock-type is still a
Rock-type. Squirtle can take it down.
Squirtle, Hydro Pump!"

Fierce streams of water shot out of the
openings in Squirtle's shell. The water
assaulted Onix from all sides. The large
Pokémon groaned and loosened its grip.

Drake's face tensed. "Onix, Dive! Evade
that Hydro Pump!"

But Onix was too wiped out to make
the move. Ash took advantage of his
opponent's weakness.

"Squirtle, Skull Bash!" Ash called out.

Squirtle popped back out of its shell. It
sped along the ground and then slammed
into Onix's head with the top of its skull.

That was all Onix could take. The Rock
Snake Pokémon's eyes closed as it sank to
the field.

"Onix is unable to battle," said the judge.

On the scoreboard, Onix's picture faded.

"It's a rockslide!" cried the announcer. "Ash's tiny turtle took down Drake's super-sized Rock Snake. I guess this kid knows what he's doing. But does he have what it takes to go all the way?"

"Good job, Squirtle!" Ash congratulated his Pokémon happily.

Drake recalled Onix. "Good job, my friend," he said quietly.

"Drake has suffered two defeats in a row," said the announcer. "What will he do now?"

Drake didn't look concerned. "How will you do against this type of Pokémon?" he asked Ash. He threw out another Poké Ball.

The ball burst open, and a purple Pokémon with orange eyes flew out.

"Gengar!" Ash cried. "A Ghost- and Poison-type Pokémon!"

Ash knew that Water-type
attacks would have no
effect on a Ghost-type
Pokémon. He held out
a Poké Ball and recalled
Squirtle.

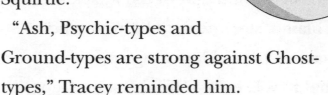

"Ash, Psychic-types and
Ground-types are strong against Ghost-
types," Tracey reminded him.

"Right!" Ash said. "Tauros can use Ground
attacks. Tauros, I choose you!"

The Wild Bull Pokémon exploded from
the ball. It snorted and pawed its giant
hoof on the ground.

"A Tauros," the announcer said. "Gengar is
immune to physical attacks. It looks like Ash
doesn't have a ghost of a chance!"

Ash gave the command. "Tauros, Fissure!"

Tauros slammed its two front legs down. The ground shook like an earthquake.

Gengar teetered dangerously back and forth. It looked like it might fall.

"Now that's power!" the announcer cried. "Gengar didn't know what hit it!"

Then the second part of the attack kicked in. A blast of energy like a lightning bolt sped across the field, tearing apart the dirt. Ash held his breath. If this blast hit Gengar, he'd win this round for sure.

"Jump, Gengar!" Drake called out.

Gengar jumped up and floated in the air. The Fissure attack passed by harmlessly underneath it.

"Gengar! Confuse Ray!" cried Drake.

Gengar turned into a transparent cloud of red gas. Red rays poured from its body.

The confusion rays hit Tauros.

Immediately, the Pokémon began slamming its horns into the boulders on the field.

"Tauros is confused," said the announcer. "It doesn't know what it's doing. It's hurting itself with its own attacks!"

Ash knew there was nothing more Tauros could do now. "Return, Tauros!" he cried.

Ash thought about his options.

*Gengar only escaped that attack because it floated away. I've got to stop it from moving. What attack can do that?*

Then Ash knew. "An Ice Beam is what I need," he said aloud. "Lapras, I choose you!"

CHAPTER 7

# LAPRAS VS GENGAR

Ash tossed a Poké Ball into the pool as he spoke. The blue-and-white Pokémon appeared in a flash of light.

The crowd "ooh"ed and "aah"ed as they watched the combination Water- and Ice-type Pokémon splash in the pool.

Drake looked a bit impressed, too, but it didn't slow him down.

"Gengar, Hypnosis!" Drake cried.

Gengar waved its arms, generating
hypnotising waves. The waves pulsated
through the air, but at Ash's command,
Lapras dived into the pool just in time
to avoid Hypnosis.

Now it was time for Ash to make an
offensive move.

"Lapras, Water Gun!" he yelled.

Lapras rose up out of the pool. It squirted
a stream of water at Gengar.

The Water Gun attack knocked the wind
out of Gengar, but it wasn't enough to take
down the Ghost- and Poison-type Pokémon.
Ash knew that. He also knew that Drake was
going to do his best to defeat Lapras before
it could do any more damage.

Ash was right.

"Gengar, Night Shade!" Drake called out.

Ash quickly came up with a counter-attack.

"Lapras, Ice Beam!"

Black beams poured from Gengar's eyes. At the same time, icy cold blue beams shot out from Lapras's eyes.

The two attacks met over the field.

*Ka-boom!* The two colliding forces created a huge explosion. Thick dust and smoke covered the field.

"Lapras!" Ash cried. Was his Pokémon OK?

The smoke slowly started to clear.

"What an explosion! Pummelo Stadium is on its feet!" cried the announcer. "Which Pokémon will be left standing?"

Now Ash could see both Lapras and Gengar. The two Pokémon were splayed out across the rocky field.

"Both of the Pokémon are knocked out!" ruled the judge.

Ash and Drake recalled their Pokémon.

"Good work, Lapras," Ash said. Lapras had fought well. It had taken down a Pokémon that was tough to beat.

Ash looked up at the scoreboard. The pictures of Lapras and Gengar both faded out. This was his first Pokémon to faint.

Thankfully, Ash knew Lapras would be better before long. Most Pokémon recovered quickly after a battle, especially after being healed at a Pokémon Center.

But this battle was far from over. He had two more Pokémon he hadn't used yet. And he could still bring out Pikachu, Squirtle and Tauros if he had to. Their pictures were still illuminated on the screen.

"That Ghost-type Pokémon battle will

haunt Drake for a long time to come," the announcer was saying. "Ash has knocked out three of Drake's Pokémon in a row. It's time for a field change."

The rock field sank back into the ground. Then a new field rose up in its place. Sand covered the flat surface of the field.

"This battle is really heating up! Our next field fits right in – a desert terrain," said the announcer. "On this field, the Pokémon will have to try to keep their footing on the unstable sand."

Ash sized up this new challenge. His Pokémon could handle it. All he had to do was take down the rest of Drake's Pokémon. Then again, that might not be so easy ...

Ash gazed up at the huge Dragonite statue that towered over the stadium. Drake was probably saving Dragonite for last. Were

Ash's Pokémon strong enough to battle such a powerful creature? He wasn't sure.

~~~

While Ash pondered his next move, three interested observers watched the action from the stands.

Jessie, James and Meowth had a new plan for stealing Pokémon. But Team Rocket wasn't after Pikachu this time.

"That Dragonite is bound to come out pretty soon," Jessie said. "We'll let that twerp weaken it, and then it will be easy for us to steal."

"But do you think that whiny wimp can beat the Dragonite?" James asked.

"He doesn't have to," Jessie reminded him. "All he has to do is wear it down."

"We may not get the Winner's Cup," Meowth added. "But when we get that Dragonite, Team Rocket will be the real winners!"

## CHAPTER 8

# ELECTABUZZ, THUNDERPUNCH

Back on the field, Drake threw a Poké Ball.

"Go, Venusaur!" he yelled.

A large blue Pokémon exploded from the ball. Venusaur was the evolved form of Bulbasaur and Ivysaur. It walked on all fours and had a huge flower on its back.

Ash thought about his strategy. Combination Grass- and Poison-type

Pokémon like Venusaur were weak against Normal-type and Rock-type Pokémon.

"Tauros, I choose you!" Ash cried.

Ash threw a Poké Ball and Tauros appeared. It seemed to have shaken the effects of the Confusion attack.

Ash didn't waste any time. "Tauros, Fissure!" he called out.

"Ash knows a good thing when he sees it," said the announcer as Tauros stomped its two strong legs into the sandy field.

Ash waited for the ground to start shaking. But instead, he watched Tauros's legs sinking into the sand.

"What's this?" asked the announcer. "The soft sand is weakening Tauros's attack! Fissure is fizzling out!"

Drake saw his chance, and took it. "Venusaur, Solar Beam!"

Venusaur started to gather concentrated beams of sunlight into its flower.

"Hit it now, Ash, while it's absorbing energy!" Tracey called out.

"Right!" Ash said. "Tauros, Take Down!"

Tauros lowered its head and started to charge Venusaur.

"Venusaur, now! Launch Solar Beam!" Drake cried out to his Pokémon.

The flower on Venusaur's back began to glow with yellow light. Tauros skidded to a stop in front of Venusaur, then tackled the Pokémon with all its might.

The attack sent Venusaur flying, but that didn't stop it from launching its Solar Beam.

The golden beam poured from the flower. Tauros tried to move out of the way, but its legs were stuck in the sand.

*Bam!* The solar blast hit Tauros, tossing the wild bull across the field.

"Please get up, Tauros," Ash pleaded.

Tauros slowly rose to its feet.

"Wow! What a twist!" said the announcer. "The Solar Beam actually freed Tauros's legs from the sand."

"All right!" Ash said. "Tauros, Take Down!"

Tauros charged at Venusaur again. At Drake's command, thick green vines unfurled from the leaves on Venusaur's back. The vines lashed at Tauros.

Tauros bravely carried on, charging through the stinging whips.

*Slam!* Tauros collided with Venusaur again. This time, Venusaur crashed to the ground.

"Tauros's Take Down finds its mark!" said the announcer.

The judge in the orange shirt made the call. "Venusaur is unable to battle!"

"Ash is on fire!" said the announcer as Venusaur's picture darkened on the scoreboard. "He's knocked out four of Drake's Pokémon in a row!"

Ash sized up the situation. Drake had two Pokémon left. Ash still had five.

Could he really beat Dragonite, even with this advantage?

Ash was going to have to wait to find out. The next Pokémon Drake called on was a yellow-and-black Electabuzz. This Pokémon had some of the most powerful Electric attacks around.

"Ash's Tauros looks tired out!" said the announcer. "Will Ash call in a replacement?"

Ash knew the
announcer had a
good point. Usually,
a Normal-type
Pokémon would
be a good
choice against
an Electric-type Pokémon. But Tauros was
pretty weak.

Ash recalled Tauros, then threw out
another Poké Ball. Bulbasaur appeared.

"Bulbasaur, as a Grass- and Poison-type,
you're strong against Electric. This battle's
ours!" Ash said confidently.

"Watch out, Ash," Tracey warned him.
"You do have the advantage by type, but
Electabuzz may have experience."

"Just watch and see," Ash replied.

Drake yelled, "Electabuzz, Thundershock!"

Bright bolts of electricity shot out of the horns on Electabuzz's horns, zapping Bulbasaur. The Pokémon shook off the jolt like it was a light rain.

"Razor Leaf!" Ash yelled.

Sharp green leaves flew out of the plant bulb on Bulbasaur's back. But the attack didn't faze Electabuzz.

"Thunderpunch!" Drake cried.

Electabuzz charged straight at Bulbasaur, then hit Bulbasaur square on the face with its fist. The powerful punch was backed by a jolt of electricity.

*Pow!* The punch took its toll. Bulbasaur fell to the ground in a faint.

"Bulbasaur is out," said the judge.

"Electabuzz's high level of experience overcame Bulbasaur's advantage as a Grass-type," said the announcer.

"Good work, Bulbasaur," Ash said, holding out a Poké Ball. "Return!"

Bulbasaur disappeared, and Ash quickly threw another ball.

"Charizard, go!"

The Fire- and Flying-type Pokémon stomped its feet. Ash knew Charizard's level was high enough to counter Electabuzz.

"Charizard, Flamethrower!" Ash called.

Charizard hurled a red-hot flame at Electabuzz. The Electric-type Pokémon jumped up, missing the attack.

"Electabuzz, Thunderpunch!" Drake commanded his Pokémon.

Electabuzz slammed its fist into Charizard, zapping the Pokémon with an electric blast. Charizard reeled.

"Electabuzz, Thunder!" More electric sparks sizzled on its horns as Electabuzz charged for the next attack.

"Charizard, fight back!" Ash cried to his Pokémon. "Use Ember!"

A tornado of swirling fire burst from Charizard's mouth. It zoomed through the air, aimed right for Electabuzz. At the same time, Electabuzz let loose a Thunderblast.

The two attacks collided in midair, avoiding both Pokémon.

"The sparks are flying!" the announcer said. "These Pokémon are a good match."

"Good work, Charizard," Ash said proudly. "Use Seismic Toss!"

"Chaaaar!" Charizard flapped its wings and flew across the field. It picked up Electabuzz and flew around in circles.

"Electabuzz, Thunderbolt!" Drake yelled.

Electabuzz's horns sparked with electricity. But it was too late.

Charizard let go of Electabuzz. The Electric-type Pokémon fell like a stone, crashing into the sandy ground.

Electabuzz was sprawled on the ground, motionless. The judge walked over and examined it.

"Electabuzz is unable to battle!" he said.

Drake recalled Electabuzz. He looked strangely calm. He took a Poké Ball off the chain around his neck. The Poké Ball grew to normal size in his hand.

"Ash is only inches away from entering the Hall of Victory," said the announcer. "But Drake's remaining Pokémon is none other than the famous..."

Drake threw out the Poké Ball. A blinding light flashed all around them.

Ash squinted from the glare. When the light faded, he could see a tall orange Pokémon with a long tail and two small wings on its back.

"Dragonite!" Drake said proudly.

## CHAPTER 9

# ENTER DRAGONITE

Dragonite lowered its head and glared menacingly at Charizard.

"Dragonite sure looks serious," Tracey said.

Ash agreed. He knew Dragonite had some serious attacks. But he couldn't let his confidence fall. He had to concentrate on the battle ahead.

"Make the first move, Charizard!" Ash told his Pokémon. "Use Flamethrower!"

Drake countered this quickly. "Dragonite, Water Gun!"

Charizard aimed a scorching flame at Dragonite. The Dragon- and Flying-type Pokémon countered with a forceful stream of water that doused the flame, and knocked over Charizard.

"Drake picked the perfect attack!" the announcer said. "Our stadium leader sure knows his stuff."

"Dragonite, Ice Beam! Now!" Drake continued the assault.

"Charizard, escape into the sky!" Ash cried.

A glowing ball of white light filled Dragonite's mouth. The Pokémon opened wide and hurled the frozen beam at Charizard. In response, Charizard flew up into the air, avoiding the attack. Dragonite flew right after it.

The battle raged in the air as Ash and Drake shouted commands from below.

Charizard tried to blast Dragonite with another Flamethrower, but Dragonite dodged out of the way. Then Charizard dodged another Ice Beam from Dragonite.

Charizard began to spin in the air, building energy with each turn. The Flame Pokémon dived down to the field, then soared up again. It slammed into Dragonite.

Dragonite faltered for a second. Charizard tried to pick up Dragonite so it could perform another Seismic Toss. But Dragonite was one step ahead. Now it slammed into the Flame Pokémon. It grabbed the weakened Charizard around the neck and pounded it into the sand.

Charizard stood still for a second. Then it slowly rose to its feet.

"Ash's Charizard has taken a lot of damage, but this Fire- and Flying-type Pokémon is burning to battle!" the announcer said.

"I've got to end this now," Ash said. "Charizard, use Dragon Rage!"

"Why not?" Drake said, smiling. "We'll use Dragon Rage, too!"

A red-hot fireball formed in Charizard's mouth. Dragonite formed a fireball, too.

Both Pokémon released the attacks. The

fireballs spiralled across the field.

*Boom!* The fireballs exploded in a shower of red sparks. Dust and sand stirred up from the field.

The dust cleared. Ash watched anxiously. *Is Charizard all right?* he wondered

Both Pokémon were still standing. They looked dirty and exhausted.

But Charizard had finally taken too much damage. The lizard Pokémon fell backwards onto the ground with a thud.

The judge came to look. "Charizard is unable to battle," he declared.

"Drake has just taken out one of Ash's strongest Pokémon!" the announcer exclaimed. "Ash's remaining Pokémon are still weak from battle. Do they have what it takes to down this Dragonite?"

Ash looked at the scoreboard nervously.

Then he threw a Poké Ball. "Squirtle, I'm counting on you!"

Squirtle popped out, ready to battle.

"Hydro Pump!" Ash cried.

Squirtle pulled its head, legs and arms into its shell. The shell spun around, shooting water from every opening.

Dragonite countered with Water Gun. The Dragon Pokémon blasted Squirtle's shell with a powerful stream of water. The shell skidded across the sand.

Squirtle popped back out. It was too weak to withstand the assault.

Ash couldn't believe it. So far he had seen Dragonite use Dragon-type attacks, plus powerful Water attacks. And it could fly. What else could this Pokémon do?

Drake chose Thunderbolt for Dragonite's next move. Dragonite hurled a mighty jolt of electricity at Squirtle. Squirtle ducked back inside its shell just in time.

"An electrifying attack from Dragonite!" shouted the announcer. "Squirtle's lucky it has that shell. But it can't hide for ever."

Squirtle came back out of its shell, ready for action. At Drake's command, Dragonite flew into the air, ready to Body Slam the turtle Pokémon.

"Squirtle, Bubble attack!" Ash ordered.

Strong bubbles shot from Squirtle's mouth. They crashed into Dragonite, causing it to fall to the ground. But they didn't stop Dragonite from slamming into Squirtle. The turtle Pokémon crashed to the ground.

"Squirtle is unable to battle," said the judge. "It is out."

"A good show from Squirtle, but not good enough," said the announcer.

Ash tried to ignore the announcer. "Thanks, Squirtle," Ash said. He recalled his Pokémon. Squirtle had weakened Dragonite. And that was important.

Ash only had two Pokémon left, Tauros and Pikachu. Who would he use next?

Before he could make a decision, a hot-air balloon decorated with a Meowth face dropped down into the open stadium.

Ash couldn't believe it. Team Rocket!

A net dropped down from the balloon,

covering Dragonite and trapping it.

"Prepare for trouble ..." Jessie said.

"... and make it double!" finished James.

They started to recite their motto, but Drake interrupted them.

"How dare you interrupt this competition?" he shouted angrily.

"You won't be so hot once we take your Dragonite," Jessie said. She turned to Ash. "Thanks for fighting so hard for us. Now taking Dragonite will be a piece of cake."

"Don't be so sure!" Drake said fiercely. "Dragonite, Skull Bash!"

Dragonite jumped up, easily breaking the net. It banged its head into Team Rocket's balloon. The balloon burst, ejected a stream of hot air and careened across the sky.

"Looks like we're off again!" Team Rocket cried as they disappeared over the horizon.

"What on earth just happened here?"
the announcer asked. "Let's get this show
back in gear."

Ash decided to save Pikachu for last.
Tauros might be stronger, but Pikachu
always came through for Ash when things
were looking hopeless.

Ash called on Tauros next. The wild
bull Pokémon jumped up and then ran
across the field.

Dragonite flew down from the sky
and crashed into Tauros. The force
drove the Pokémon's legs deep into
the sand. Tauros was stuck.

"It's like quicksand out there," said the
announcer. That didn't stop Tauros from
charging ahead. It grabbed Dragonite with
its horns and slammed it on to the field.

"That's a good strategy," Tracey remarked.

"Usually Tauros takes damage when it uses its ground attacks. But the sand is cushioning the backlash."

"Don't give in," Drake told Dragonite. "Use Thunder attack!"

Dragonite shocked Tauros with a sizzling jolt of electricity. The weakened Pokémon succumbed to the attack. Tauros's knees buckled, and it collapsed in the sand.

"Tauros is unable to battle!" said the judge.

"Ash is now down to his last Pokémon," said the announcer. "The pride of Pummelo Stadium is unstoppable!"

Ash looked down by his side. Sparks sizzled on Pikachu's red cheeks. It was eager to take the challenge.

"You're all I have left, Pikachu," Ash said. "It's up to you!"

## CHAPTER 12

# PIKACHU VS DRAGONITE

"Ash's final Pokémon is Pikachu," said the announcer. "Pikachu is still weak from its battle with Ditto. Will the Lightning Mouse Pokémon prevail over this Devastating Dragon Pokémon?"

Ash was betting it would.

"Go, Pikachu!" Ash cried.

Pikachu jumped towards Dragonite. The Dragon-type Pokémon smacked Pikachu with its strong tail. Pikachu flew backwards across the field and landed on its back.

"Hang in there, Pikachu!" Tracey and Misty cheered from the stands.

Dragonite clearly had the advantage. "Use Hyper Beam!" Drake commanded.

Dragonite gathered energy. A ball of golden light formed in its mouth.

"I can't look!" said the announcer. "Hyper Beam is Dragonite's strongest attack. It looks like Pikachu has met its match!"

"Pikachu, use Agility!" Ash called out. He watched helplessly as the Hyper Beam spun from Dragonite's mouth. Blinding golden light exploded across the field.

"Pikachu!" Ash cried out.

The light faded. Ash expected to see that

Pikachu had fainted from the attack.

But it hadn't.

Pikachu soared high above the field, looking strong and confident.

The announcer figured out what had happened. "Incredible! Pikachu jumped, using its tail as a springboard. It escaped the Hyper Beam!"

Pikachu landed on top of Dragonite's head. The larger Pokémon panted heavily.

"Dragonite used up its energy in that last attack!" said the announcer. "It can't move!"

Dragonite tried to shake off Pikachu. But it just couldn't do it. It was too weak. The Dragon Pokémon even tried to bury its head in the sand. But Pikachu held fast.

"Pikachu's speed and agility are coming in handy right now," said the announcer. "But wait until Dragonite gets its energy back!"

"Pikachu's got to do something soon, or it'll be in real trouble!" Misty remarked.

Ash knew just what to do. "Pikachu, Thunder!" he yelled.

"Pikachuuuuuu!" Pikachu unleashed a ferocious electric charge at Dragonite. The Dragon-type Pokémon's whole body lit up.

Dragonite cried out. It finally shook off Pikachu, tossing the Electric-type Pokémon

a few feet away.

Pikachu quickly jumped to its feet. Dragonite stomped towards Pikachu.

The two Pokémon faced off.

Ash wondered what his next move should be. Pikachu was looking just as exhausted as Dragonite.

Ash didn't have to decide. Dragonite's eyes fluttered. It rocked back and forth. Finally, the powerful Pokémon toppled back, crashing on to the field.

The judge made his final ruling. "Dragonite is unable to battle," he said. "Victory goes to Ash!"

"He did it!" the announcer shouted. "Ash is the first challenger to defeat Drake!"

Pikachu jumped into Ash's arms. Tracey and Misty ran on to the field. Ash released his other Pokémon, too. They all cheered and hugged one another.

Ash was really proud of his team. They had all worked together, using their combined skills to wear down Dragonite.

Ash broke away from his friends and walked towards Drake.

"Congratulations, Ash," Drake said, smiling. "That was an awesome match. It's an honour to lose to a challenger like you."

"Thanks," Ash said. "That's some Dragonite you have there. It was an honour to battle you, too."

Drake smiled. "Now it's time to take your place in the Palace of Victory!"

By the next day, a picture of Ash and his Pokémon had a permanent place in the hall. The Pokémon had all put their footprints on a cement slab, and the footprints were now displayed there, too.

Ash stared at the picture. He couldn't believe it. He had actually won the Winner's Cup. It seemed like ages ago that he had made the decision to try for it.

"You did a great job in that battle, Ash," Tracey told him.

Usually Misty hated to admit when Ash did anything right, but even she had to agree. "I'm really proud of you," she said.

### The End

FIND OUT HOW ASH AND
FRIENDS' ADVENTURES ON
THE ORANGE ISLANDS BEGAN IN

# ASH'S BIG CHALLENGE

READ ON FOR A SNEAK PEEK ...

"Ash, I need you to run a very important errand for me," Professor Oak said.

Ash Ketchum beamed. Here he was back in Pallet Town in the lab of Professor Oak, one of the world's greatest Pokémon experts. He was surrounded by his best friends, Misty and Brock. Pikachu, his favourite Pokémon, sat on his shoulder. And now Professor Oak was entrusting him with an important mission. Ash felt proud.

"Of course, I asked my grandson Gary to

go," Professor Oak said, "but he was busy."

Ash cringed. He should have guessed he was second choice after Gary. Gary had begun his Pokémon training at the same time as Ash and was his top rival.

"What's the errand?" Misty asked.

"I need you to go to Valencia Island in the Orange Archipelago," Professor Oak said.

"The Archipela-who?" Ash asked.

But Misty and Brock looked excited.

"Valencia! It's beautiful there," Misty said.

"Yeah," Brock said. "And there are lots of girls on the beach."

"My friend Professor Ivy works there," the professor continued. "She recently acquired a mysterious Poké Ball. I'd like you to bring it to me so that I can study it."

"Can't you just have her transport it to you like any other Poké Ball, Professor?" Misty asked. Trainers from Pallet Town often transported Pokémon in their Poké Balls to Professor Oak's lab. Because Trainers can only carry six Pokémon at a time, he helped them raise any extra Pokémon they caught.

"We've tried to transport the Poké Ball, but it doesn't work," Professor Oak said. "That's one of the reasons it's so mysterious."

Ash liked the sound of that. "Of course I'll go, Professor," he said.

"Me, too," said Misty and Brock together.

Professor Oak smiled. "Wonderful!" he said. "I know I can count on all of you."

Ash and his friends started out on their journey the next morning. Brock carried a pack filled with special Pokémon food. Brock looked tough, but he knew a lot about caring for Pokémon.

Misty held Togepi, her baby Pokémon. Pikachu walked alongside Ash. Its lightning-bolt tail bobbed up and down. They trekked through the forest in silence, but Ash's mind was crowded with thoughts.

Ash was ten years old when he first began his journey as a Pokémon Trainer in Professor Oak's lab. A lot had happened since then. He had fought Gym Leaders in eight different towns and earned badges from all of them. He had even competed in the Pokémon League, where he finished in the top sixteen. Not bad.

And most important, he was learning how to become a good Pokémon Trainer. He had caught and trained many different types of Pokémon. Some of them had even evolved into higher forms. Charmander had evolved into Charmeleon and then

Charizard. Pidgey, his Flying-type Pokémon, had recently evolved into Pidgeot.

Ash was learning more each day. And now Professor Oak had entrusted him with an important mission. He couldn't wait!

Ash and his friends walked for hours. Eventually, Ash saw the crystal blue ocean twinkling in the sunlight.

"All right!" Ash said. "We'll be on Valencia Island in no time."

Brock flipped through a guidebook. He frowned.

"I've got bad news, Ash," Brock said. "According to this, we'll have to sail for weeks to get anywhere near the island!"

"Weeks!" Ash cried.

Brock flipped through the book. "If we go by blimp, it will take less than a day," he said. "But the blimp is pretty expensive."

Ash turned out his pockets. He had a few coins but not enough for a blimp ride.

"I wish we had enough money to go by blimp," Ash said. "Don't you, Pikachu?"

"Pika!" The yellow Electric-type Pokémon nodded in agreement.

Ash sighed. "I'd better go buy some food and supplies for our trip," he said.

READ
ASH'S BIG CHALLENGE
TO FIND OUT WHAT HAPPENS NEXT!

# POKÉ RAP!

I want to be the very best there ever was
To beat all the rest, yeah, that's my cause
Catch 'em, Catch 'em, Gotta catch 'em all
Pokémon I'll search across the land
Look far and wide
Release from my hand
The power that's inside
Catch 'em, Catch 'em, Gotta catch 'em all Pokémon!
Gotta catch 'em all, Gotta catch 'em all
Gotta catch 'em all, Gotta catch 'em all
At least one hundred and fifty or more to see
To be a Pokémon Master is my destiny
Catch 'em, Catch 'em, Gotta catch 'em all
Gotta catch 'em all, Pokémon! (repeat three times)

# CAN YOU RAP ALL 150?
## HERE'S THE NEXT 32 POKÉMON.

Alakazam, Goldeen, Venonat, Machoke

Kangaskhan, Hypno, Electabuzz, Flareon

Blastoise, Poliwhirl, Oddish, Drowzee

Raichu, Nidoqueen, Bellsprout, Starmie

Metapod, Marowak, Kakuna, Clefairy

Dodrio, Seadra, Vileplume, Krabby

Lickitung, Tauros, Weedle, Nidoran

Machop, Shellder, Porygon, Hitmonchan.

Words and Music by Tamara Loeffler and John Siegler
Copyright © 1999 Pikachu Music (BMI)
Worldwide rights for Pikachu Music administered by Cherry River Music Co. (BMI)
All Rights Reserved                    Used by Permission

## WHICH POKÉMON DID YOU
## FIND IN THIS ADVENTURE?

☐ GENGAR      ☐ TAUROS      ☐ DITTO

Find information on these and all the other Pokémon
in the Official Pokémon Encyclopedia!